THE SENSE OF
TOUCH
A First Look

PERCY LEED

Lerner Publications ◆ Minneapolis

Educator Toolbox

Reading books is a great way for kids to express what they're interested in. Before reading this title, ask the reader these questions:

What do you think this book is about? Look at the cover for clues.

What do you already know about touch?

What do you want to learn about touch?

Let's Read Together

Encourage the reader to use the pictures to understand the text.

Point out when the reader successfully sounds out a word.

Praise the reader for recognizing sight words such as *my* and *with*.

TABLE OF CONTENTS

Touch 4

Touch

Touch is one of my senses.

When I touch,
I feel with my skin.

What else does
your skin do?

I feel something hard.
I feel a bat.
I feel a shell.

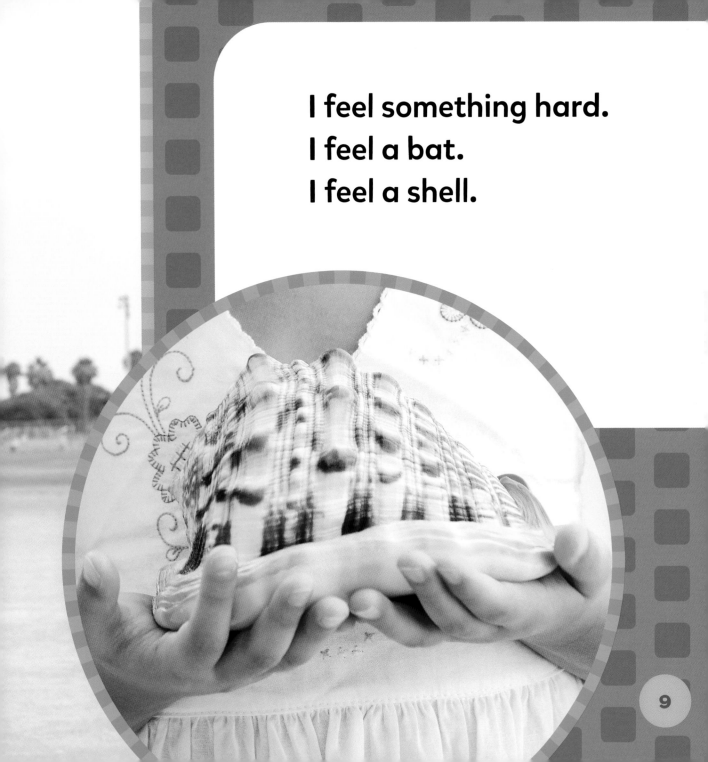

I feel something soft.
I feel a blanket.

I feel fur.

I feel something smooth.
I feel a slide.

I feel paint.

I feel something rough.
I feel pine cones.
I feel a tree.

What other things feel rough?

15

I feel something hot.
I feel bathwater.
I feel sand in the sun.

I feel something cold.
I feel snow.

I feel ice cream.

I touch many things.
What do you touch?

You Connect!

What is your favorite thing to touch?

What is something you don't like to touch?

What other senses do you know about?

STEM Snapshot

Encourage students to think and ask questions like scientists. Ask the reader:

What is something you learned about touch?

What is something you noticed about touch?

What is something you still want to learn about touch?

Photo Glossary

fur

pine cone

shell

skin

Learn More

Leed, Percy. *The Sense of Sight: A First Look*. Minneapolis: Lerner Publications, 2023.

Ransom, Candice F. *Let's Explore the Five Senses*. Minneapolis: Lerner Publications, 2020.

Rebman, Nick. *Touch*. Lake Elmo, MN: Focus Readers, 2022.

Index

Photo Acknowledgments

The images in this book are used with the permission of: © Asia Images Group/Shutterstock Images, pp. 9, 23 (shell); © fstop123/iStockphoto, p. 13; © Huang Henry SH/Shutterstock Images, p. 18; © Image Source/iStockphoto, pp. 11, 23 (fur); © jarabee123/Shutterstock Images, pp. 6–7, 23 (skin); © LightFieldStudios/iStockphoto, pp. 14, 23 (pine cone); © manley099/iStockphoto, p. 12; © monkeybusinessimages/iStockphoto, pp. 8–9; © nortonrsx/iStockphoto, p. 10; © PradeepGaurs/Shutterstock Images, pp. 4–5; © SolStock/iStockphoto, pp. 14–15; © StockImageFactory.com/Shutterstock Images, p. 19; © Suzanne Tucker/Shutterstock Images, p. 17; © Tanongsak Sangthong/Shutterstock Images, pp. 16–17; © yupiyan/iStockphoto, p. 20.

Cover Photos: © ESB Professional/Shutterstock Images (girl and dog), mouu007/Shutterstock Images (background texture), MM_photos/Shutterstock Images (background texture).

Design Elements: © Mighty Media, Inc.

Lerner Publications Company
An imprint of Lerner Publishing Group, Inc.
241 First Avenue North
Minneapolis, MN 55401 USA

For reading levels and more information, look up this title at www.lernerbooks.com.

Main body text set in Mikado a Medium.
Typeface provided by Hannes von Doehren.

Library of Congress Cataloging-in-Publication Data

Library of Congress Cataloging-in-Publication Data

Names: Leed, Percy, 1968– author.
Title: The sense of touch : a first look / Percy Leed.
Description: Minneapolis : Lerner Publications, [2023] | Series: Read about senses (read for a better world) | Includes bibliographical references and index. | Audience: Ages 5–8 | Audience: Grades K–1 | Summary: "We feel with our skin. Accessible text and questions to build connections give early learners an engaging first look at the sense of touch"– Provided by publisher.
Identifiers: LCCN 2021051354 (print) | LCCN 2021051355 (ebook) | ISBN 9781728459202 (library binding) | ISBN 9781728464305 (paperback) | ISBN 9781728462035 (ebook)
Subjects: LCSH: Touch—Juvenile literature.
Classification: LCC QP451 .L44 2023 (print) | LCC QP451 (ebook) | DDC 612.8/8—dc23/eng/20211020

LC record available at https://lccn.loc.gov/2021051354
LC ebook record available at https://lccn.loc.gov/2021051355

Manufactured in the United States of America
1 – CG – 7/15/22